MY MANY COLOURED DAYS

Dr Seuss wrote this text in 1973, inspired by the panoramic view of the ocean from his study. He stated in a letter that it 'needed a great colour artist who would not be dominated by me and who would bring a new pattern of thinking to my words'. After his death in 1991 his widow brought it to the attention of his editor who commissioned these remarkable paintings from Steve Johnson and Lou Fancher.

MY MANY COLOURED DAYS

by Dr. Seuss

paintings by

STEVE JOHNSON AND LOU FANCHER

RED FOX

Some days are yellow.

Some are blue.

On different days
I'm different **too.**

You'd be
surprised
how many ways

I change
on Different
Coloured
Days.

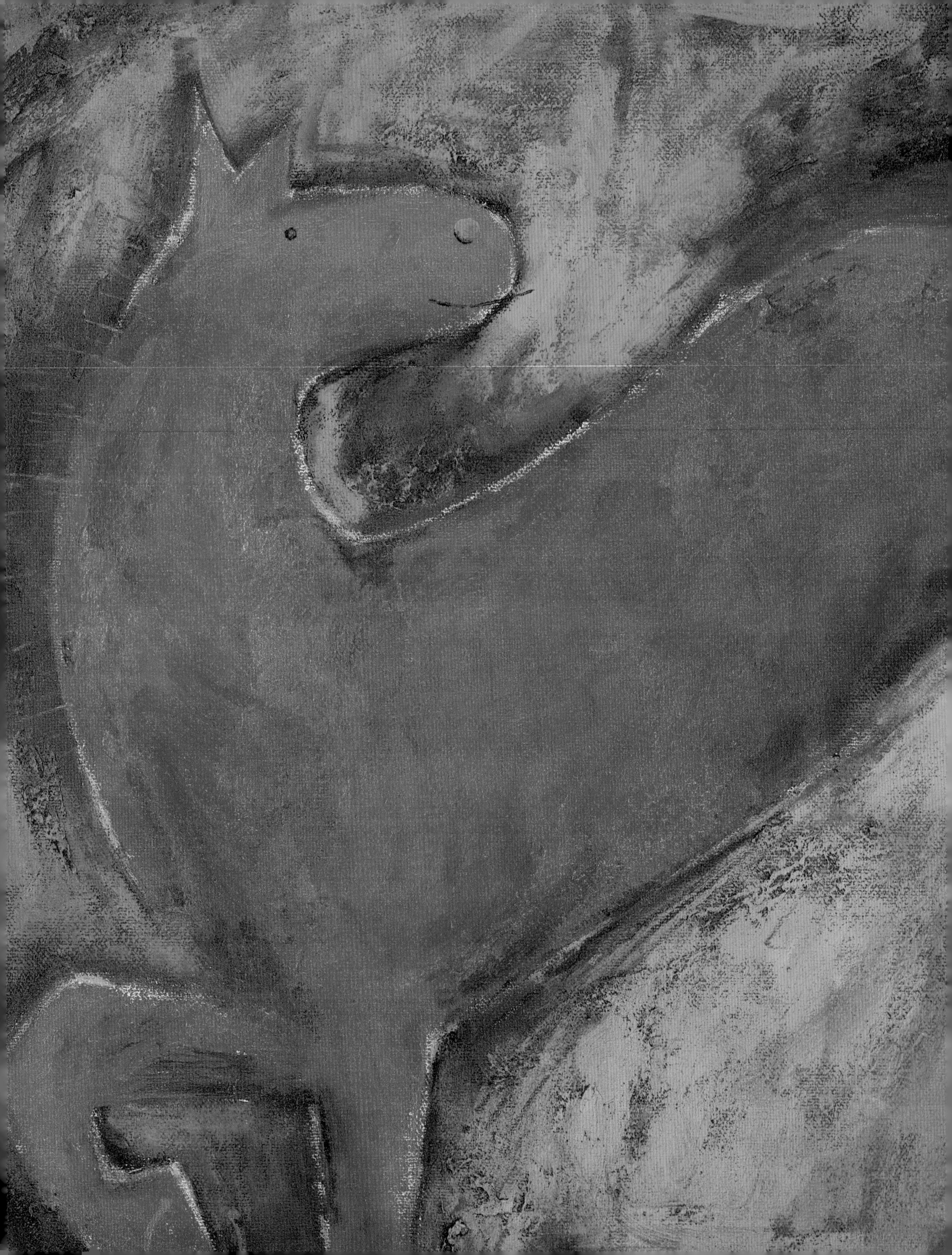

On Bright Red Days
how **good** it feels
to be a horse
and kick my heels!

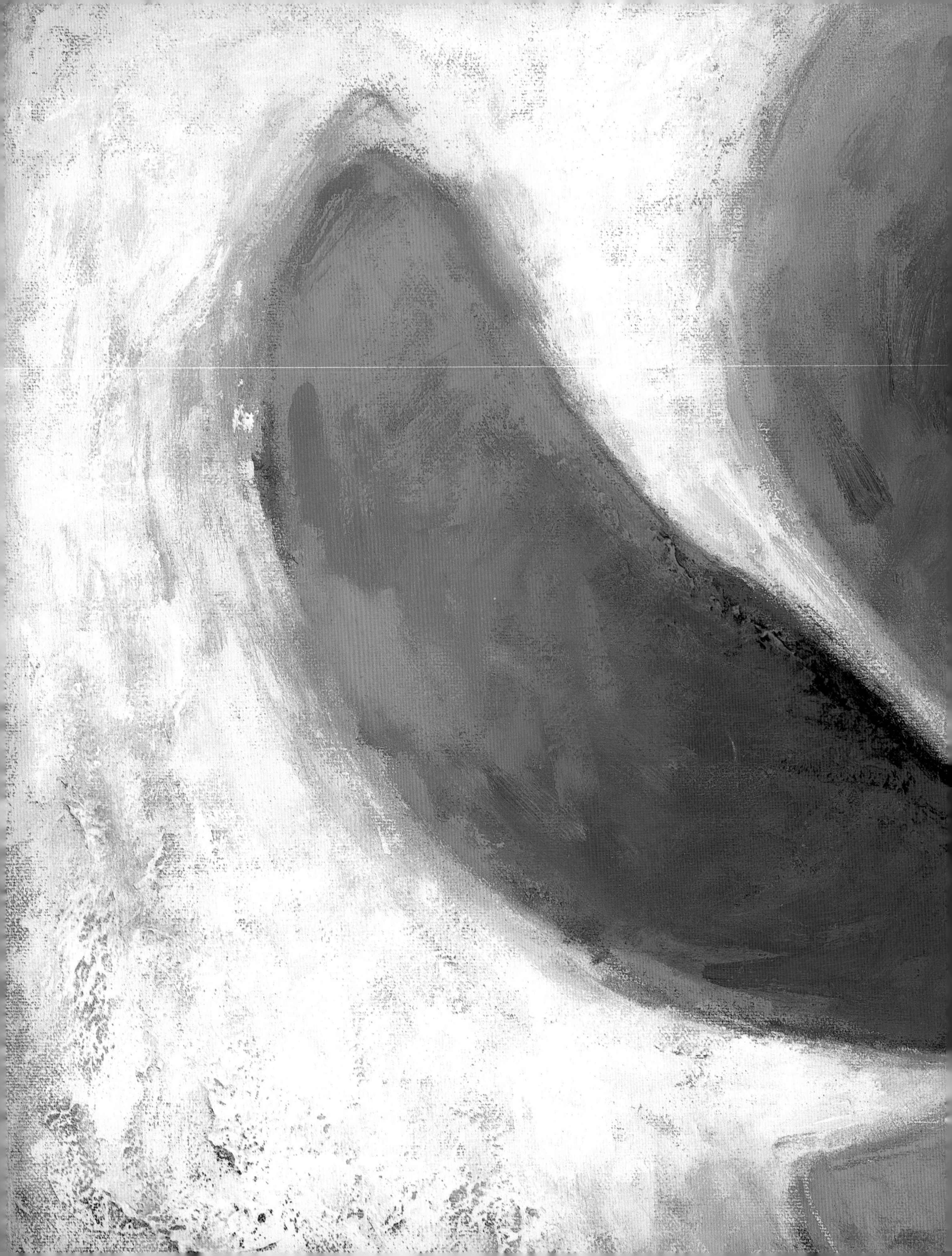

On other days I'm other things.

On Bright Blue Days

I flap my wings.

Some days, of course,
feel sort of Brown.

Then I feel slow
and low,
low
down.

Then comes a Yellow Day.

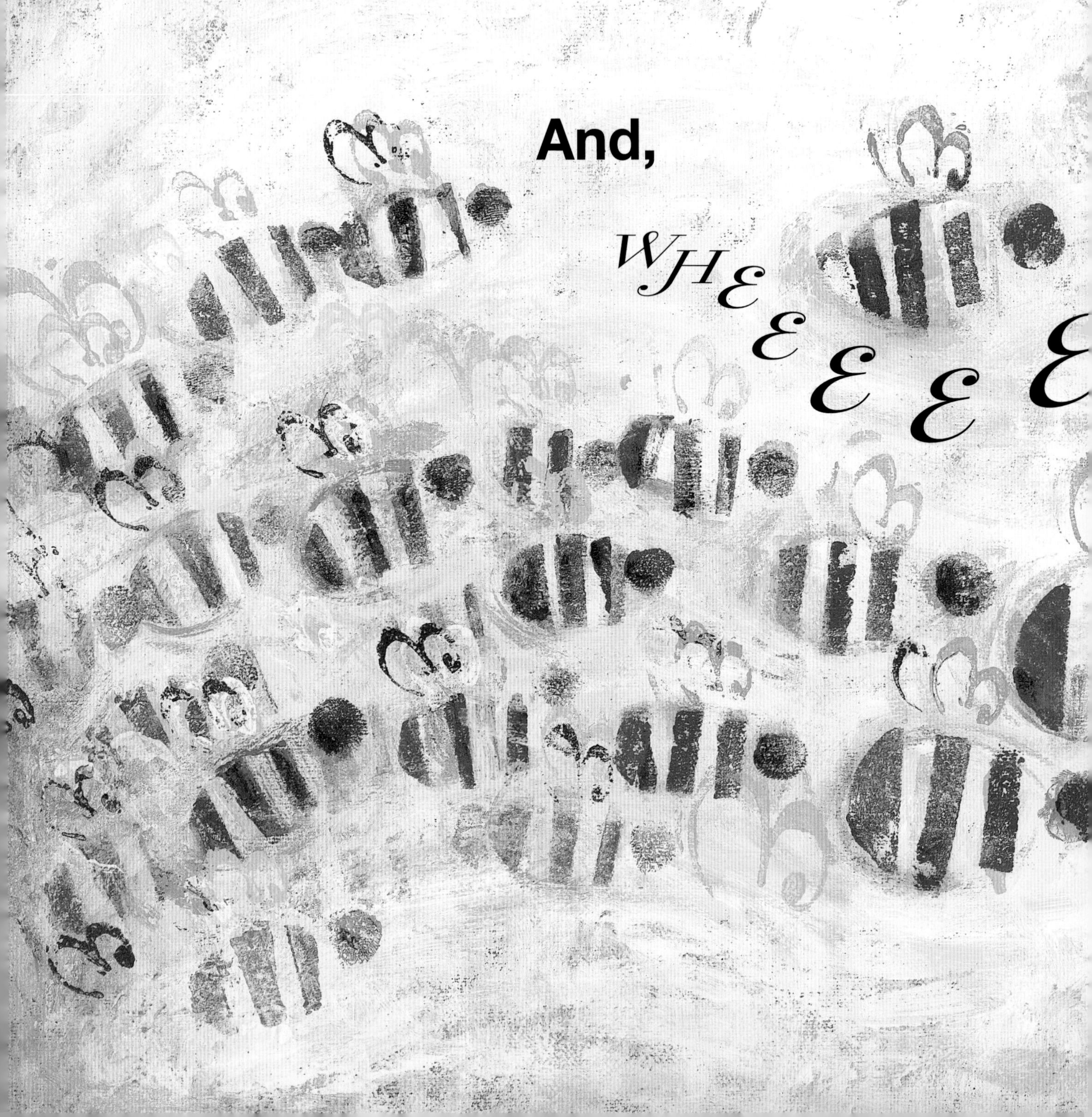

And,

WHEEEEE

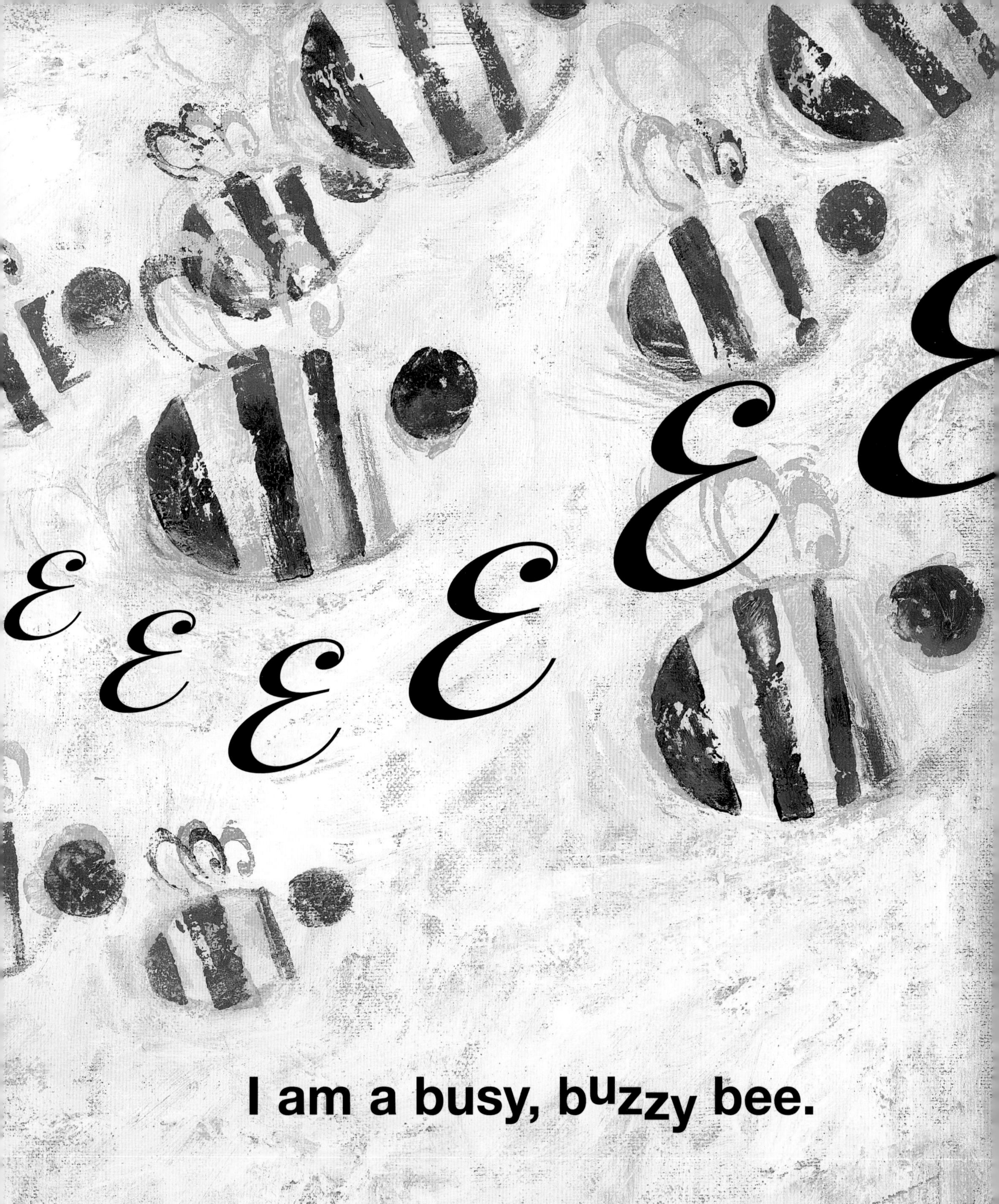

I am a busy, buzzy bee.

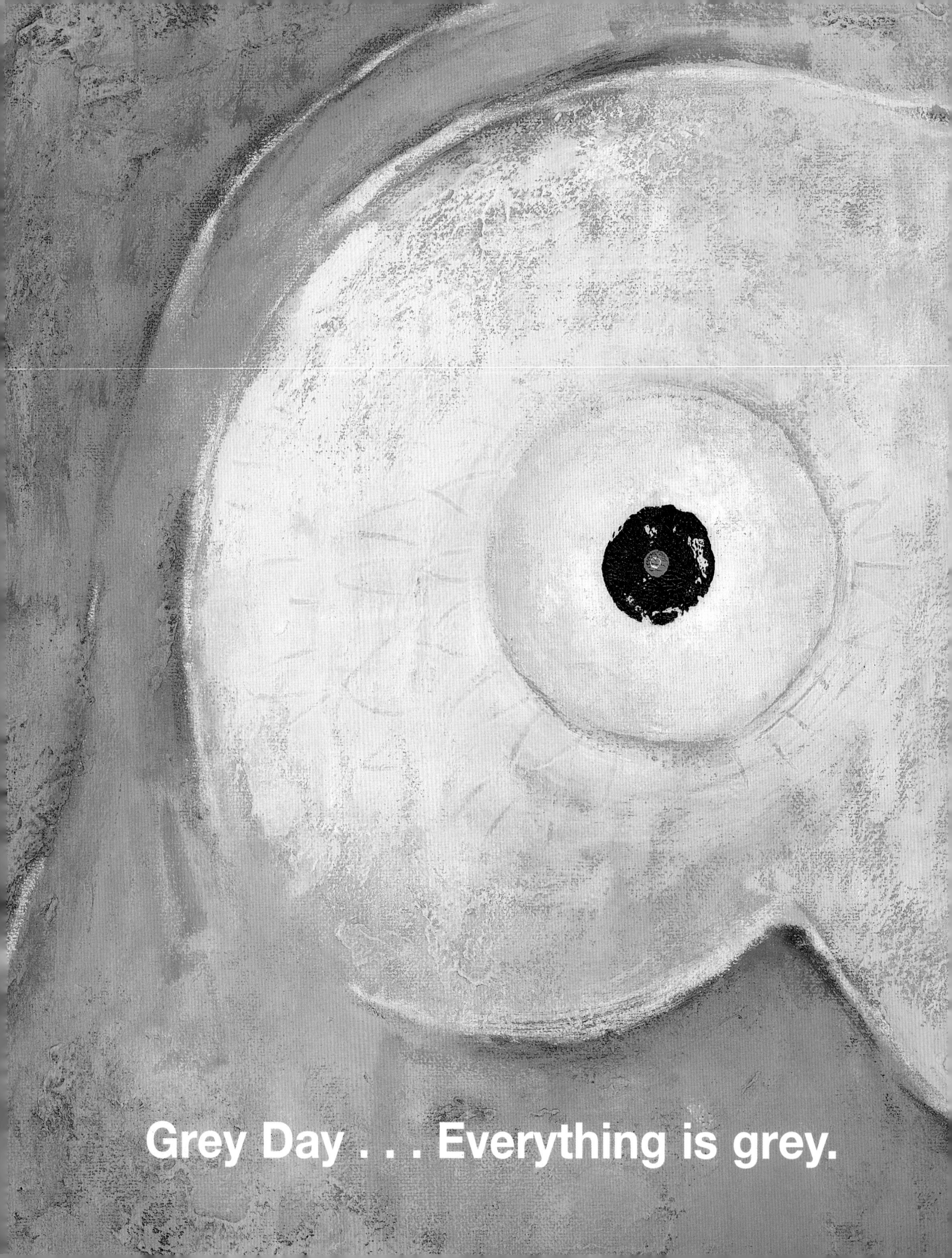
Grey Day . . . Everything is grey.

I watch. But nothing moves today.

Then
all of a sudden

I'm a

circus seal!

On my Orange Days
that's how I feel.

Green Days. **Deep deep** in the sea.

Cool and quiet **fish. That's me.**

On Purple Days

I'm sad.

I *groan.*

I drag my tail.

I walk alone.

But when my days
are Happy
Pink

jump
it's great to
and just not think.

Then come my **Black Days.**

MAD. And **loud**.

I howl.

I growl at every cloud.

Then comes a Mixed-Up Day.
And WHAM!

I don't know
who
or what
I am!

But it all turns out all right, you see.

And I go back
to being . . .
me.

To Ted, who coloured my days...and my life.

—Audrey Geisel

For Denise and Frances.

—Steve Johnson and Lou Fancher

A Red Fox Book

Published by Random House Children's Books
20 Vauxhall Bridge Road, London SW1V 2SA

A division of The Random House Group Ltd
London Melbourne Sydney Auckland
Johannesburg and agencies throughout the world

1 3 5 7 9 10 8 6 4 2

First published in the United States by Alfred A. Knopf, Inc in 1996
First published in Great Britain by Hutchinson Children's Books 1998
Red Fox edition 2001

Printed in Hong Kong

THE RANDOM HOUSE GROUP Limited Reg. No. 954009

www.randomhouse.co.uk

ISBN 0 09 926659 8